THIS BLOOMSBURY BOOK

BELONGS TO

....

Bloomsbury Publishing, London, Berlin, New York and Sydney

First published in Great Britain in June 2011 by Bloomsbury Publishing Plc
36 Soho Square, London, W1D 3QY

First published as *Chaos in Bad Berleburg* in Germany in 2010 by Jacoby & Stuart GmbH
Straßburger Straße 11, 10405 Berlin

Copyright © Verlagshaus Jacoby & Stuart GmbH, Berlin, Germany 2010
English translation copyright © Bloomsbury Publishing Plc 2011
English translation by Daniela Bernardelle
The moral rights of the author/illustrator and the translator have been asserted

A CIP catalogue record of this book is available from the British Library

ISBN 978 1 4088 0939 6

1 3 5 7 9 10 8 6 4 2

Printed in China by Toppan Leefung Printing Ltd, Dongguan, Guangdong

www.bloomsbury.com

Banana
Skin Chaos!

Lilli L'Arronge

BLOOMSBURY

LONDON BERLIN NEW YORK SYDNEY

Hubert eats all of his banana.
Well, almost all of it.
He doesn't eat the skin, of course —
he throws it on the ground.

YOU CAN'T
DO THAT!

WHY NOT?

JUST THINK WHAT MIGHT HAPPEN!

IT'S NOT FUNNY!

ALL SORTS OF THINGS COULD GO WRONG!

ONE THING LEADS TO ANOTHER . . . .

BEFORE YOU KNOW IT ...

Lilli L'Arronge,
born in March 1979,
loves cats, pigs and slobs.
She currently eats a
banana every morning
at 11 o'clock.
Unfortunately she's
allergic to apples.

🍌 What happens to the balloons?

🍌 Why does the blue van swerve?

🍌 Where does the cat go?

🍌 Why is the butcher chasing the pigs?

🍌 Why is the nun sitting on the bus stop sign?

🍌 Where does the cake end up?

🍌 What happens to the pot of rubbish?

🍌 Why is the snake so tubby?

🍌 Who finds love?